LUCY RIGG'S NAUGHTY PIG

By
Jacqueline H. Faber

Illustrated by
N.D. Engleson

Writers' Branding
(877) 608-6550
www.writersbranding.com
media@writersbranding.com

Dedication

Thanks to my patient editor and lifelong friend, Jerry, for editing and inspiring—*Lucy Rigg's Naughty Pig*. Thanks too to his Pappy who called cats "Meowtners," and lambs "Tambams." Blessings to Mindy for her love.

Thanks to my great illustrator, N.D. Engleson, who grew up on a ranch with a love for animals and an ability to bring them to life through his art. This is his 2nd picture book.

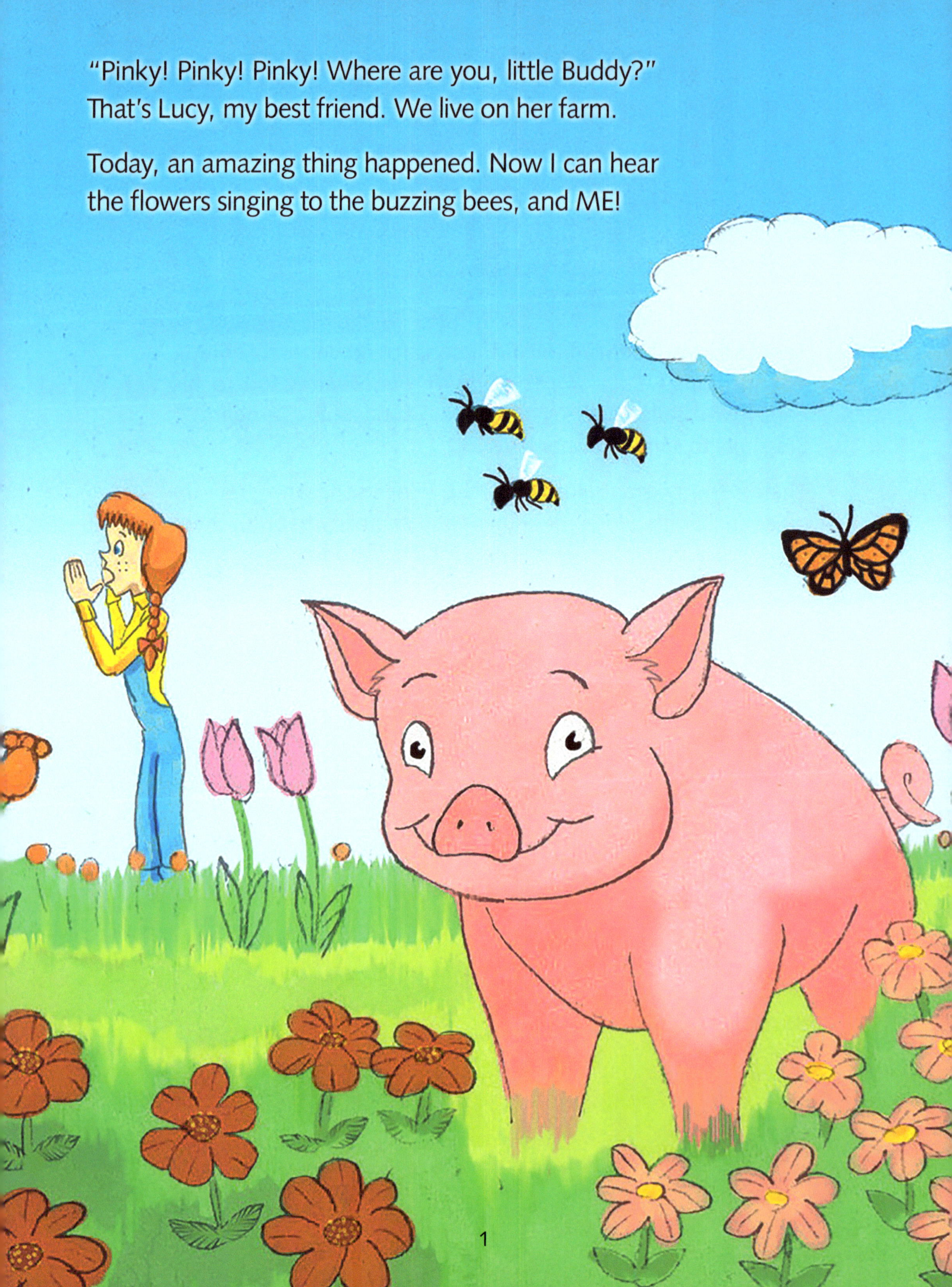

"Pinky! Pinky! Pinky! Where are you, little Buddy?"
That's Lucy, my best friend. We live on her farm.

Today, an amazing thing happened. Now I can hear
the flowers singing to the buzzing bees, and ME!

1

The Tulips trill, "We're tasty and tangy."

The Pansies croon, "We're sweet as candy."

The Chocolate Cosmos chant, "We're yummier than melted marshmallows."

So I eat all three. Yum!

"PLEASE pick me!" The begonias, buttercups, and roses sing, "Me!" "No, me!" "No meee!"

Roses tickle my nose—Aaaah CHOO! I pig out. Best Rose Petal Pudding Pie ever!

"Flowers are not for pigs," says Lucy. "They feed the birds, butterflies, and bees."

But the purple petunias are very persuasive. "Aren't we the prettiest patooties?"

"You naughty pig!" says Lucy. "Off to your pigpen."

The flowers sing on, "Sip us once! Sip us twice! Sip us once again!"

I root under the fence.

8

"Pinky! You pesky pig!" says Lucy. "How did you escape?"

Harry Hayneigh nickers, "Put him in the stall next to mine."

"Great idea, Harry. That'll pen our porky pal!"

But dreaming of a tasty rose, tickles my taste buds.
BLAM! BLAM! BLAM!

I roll in the mud, scratch my ginormous rear, and trot to the roses.

"No! No! Not my rare Rosa Rugosas!" Lucy cries. "They're the bees' favorites."

"Follow him," bleats Lily Tambam. "If he eats one more, tie him up."

Lucy tags along to my mud puddle, then the pond, then back to the garden. I don't eat a single rose, but she ties me up anyway!

13

WRIGGLE—SQUIGGLE—WAGGLE! Free again!

Lucy's tattle-tale cat Missy Meowtner spots me. "Put Pinky in the house. He can't get in trouble in here."

Lucy hoses me off and drags me…

...into her bedroom.

"Keep an eye on him, Missy."

"You can count on me," she meows.

CHOMP, CHOMP, CHOMP.
"Yuk! These daisies are dry!"
COUGH, COUGH, COUGH!
"These tulips are tasteless!"

Oh, look! My favorite—Cosmos!
"Noooooo! You nincompoop pig! Shoo!
What am I going to do with you?"
Yuck!

The next morning...

What's up? Are these for me?

My snout snorts with delight—bowls of begonias for breakfast?

For lunch, I pounce on piles of poppies.

For dinner, I grunt down platters of petunias.

For three days—breakfast, lunch, and dinner—I am in hog heaven.

But today I can't eat another blossom!

Lucy tickles a rose under my snout.

I squeeeal. "Pleeeeeease—no more flowers!"

The next morning, Lucy serves me corn and slops.

Awesomesauce! I belch a boisterous BURP! I'll never eat another blossom. "Pinky promise!"

"Look, Pinky! The birds, butterflies and bees are back!
Aren't you glad you didn't eat all their flowers? Even
when you're naughty, Pinky, I still love you!"

I grunt.

I snort.

I nudge her with my snout.

But wait!

The Cosmos are singing me their sweet song.

They always were my favorite!

29

Hmmm…

Maaaaybe…

Just one—for dessert.

Pig Trivia

Pigs are clean animals. If possible, they don't poop where they eat and sleep.

Pigs have large heads with long or short snouts. Their snouts are sensitive to touch but at the same time tough as shovels.

When pigs use their snouts to dig for food, we call this instinctual behavior rooting. It's no surprise that some of their favorite foods are roots, but they'll eat anything – animal or vegetable. With forty-four teeth, pigs forage on their own for leaves, stems, roots, fruits, flowers and grubs.

Pigs have such a keen sense of smell, gourmet suppliers train them to root for rare and expensive truffles which grow underground.

Pigs have four toes called hooves on each foot—two larger ones in front and two smaller ones behind.

Without sweat glands, pigs shed heat by wallowing in mud or water.

A pig's intelligence is on par with dogs, with whom they make friends. They get along well with cats too.

Mother pigs, called sows, build nests by rooting out a hole, then filling it with leaves or straw. This is where they give birth to their litters of 7 to 22 piglets.

Farmers must clear their fields of pig-poisonous plants like Hemlock, Nightshade, Foxglove, Angel Trumpet, Buttercups, Arum Lilies, Ragwort, Tulips, Scillas, and Hyacinths. (Pinky would not be able to eat any of these flowers!)

Mother pigs have more than 20 distinct grunts and squeals to communicate with their piglets. Newborn piglets soon learn to run towards their mother's voice. The mothers even sing to their nursing piglets.

Pigs are social animals and enjoy belly rubs from their human caretakers. Pigs use trees to rub and scratch their itches.

Pigs have such excellent sense of direction, they can navigate their way home over long distances.